Moldylocks
and the
Three Beards

Read more of Princess Pink's adventures!

1 Moldylocks and the Three Beards

2 Little Red Quacking Hood

Princess Pink AND THE LAND OF FAKE-BELIEVE

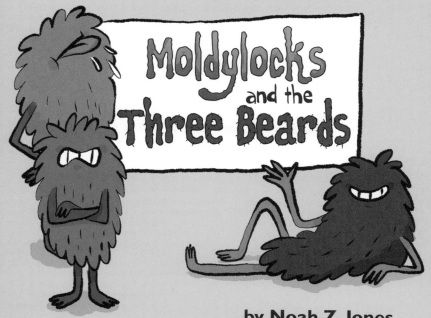

Moldylocks
and the
Three Beards

by Noah Z. Jones

BRANCHES

SCHOLASTIC INC.

FOR ELI AND SYLVIE

No part of this publication may be reproduced, stored in a retrieval system, or transmitted in any form or by any means, electronic, mechanical, photocopying, recording, or otherwise, without written permission of the publisher. For information regarding permission, write to Scholastic Inc., Attention: Permissions Department, 557 Broadway, New York, NY 10012.

Library of Congress Cataloging-in-Publication Data

Jones, Noah (Noah Z.), author.
Moldylocks and the three beards / by Noah Z. Jones.
pages cm. — (Princess Pink and the Land of Fake-Believe ; #1)
Summary: After falling through the refrigerator into the Land of Fake Believe, Princess meets a girl named Moldylocks who takes her to the home of the Three Beards for chili—but when the Beards capture her friend, Princess must come up with a plan to save her.
ISBN 978-0-545-63839-5 (pbk.) — ISBN 978-0-545-63840-1 (hardcover) — ISBN 978-0-545-63892-0 (ebook) 1. Fairy tales. 2. Humorous stories. [1. Fairy tales. 2. Humorous stories.] I. Title.
PZ8.J539Mo 2014
[E]—dc23
2013027613
ISBN 978-0-545-63840-1 (hardcover) / ISBN 978-0-545-63839-5 (paperback)

Copyright © 2014 by Noah Z. Jones

12 11 10 9 8 7 6 5 4   19 20 21 22 23/0

Printed in China   62
First Scholastic printing, January 2014

Book design by Will Denton

◇ TABLE OF CONTENTS ◇

· CHAPTER ONE ·
Meet Princess

This is Princess Pink. Her first name is <u>Princess</u>. Her last name is <u>Pink</u>.

Princess Pink does not like fairies. She does not like princesses. And she REALLY does not like the color pink.

Princess Pink <u>does</u> like dirty sneakers, giant bugs, mud puddles, monster trucks, and cheesy pizza.

Her parents named her <u>Princess</u> because they were so excited to finally have a baby girl. Princess has seven older brothers.

Penn

Paddy

Paul

Pete

Parker

Phillip

Perry

After tucking in her seven sons, Princess's mother peeked her head into Princess's room.

The fairy princess dress had been cut
into thin ribbons and taped together in
places. Princess had even colored it in
with a brown marker.

Princess's mother sighed. She did not know what to say. So she just said, "Good night, my little cowboy caveman."

Princess's mother turned off the light.

Princess's tummy made a funny
grumbly noise.

GRUMBLE
GRUMBLE

Whoa, tummy. Don't
worry! I will hunt down
something yummy
for you.

Princess tiptoed down the hallway and slipped into the kitchen. She was about to open the refrigerator, but then stopped.

The fridge always made a <u>**HUMMmmm**</u> sound—like a cat purring. But the fridge wasn't humming now. Princess put her ear to the fridge. She heard the strangest sound.

TWEET
TWEET!

Thinking that a bird had somehow gotten stuck in the fridge, Princess yanked the door open. Instead of green-bean casserole, Princess saw green rolling hills and soft white clouds.

Wow!

A giant purple polka-dotted bird was flying across a sunny sky—inside Princess's fridge! Princess leaned WAY in to get a better look.

Then she fell right through her fridge!

CHAPTER TWO
Falling Down, Down, Down

Princess did not remember falling. She also did not remember landing on a moose.

The moose prodded his hat back into its proper shape.

NO! I'm a moose with an <u>M</u>, not a goose with a <u>G</u>. <u>Mother</u> just happens to be my first name. And you are?

I'm Princess Pink. But I'm not a princess. <u>Princess</u> just happens to be my first name.

Am I still inside my refrigerator?

No. Yes. Well, maybe. You are in the Land of Fake-Believe.

A girl came running over. She had just seen Princess fall from the sky.

Are you guys okay? I'm Moldylocks! Who are you?

Moldylocks? That name doesn't sound quite right.

I'm Princess.

Princess thought Moldylocks looked like she had slept in a swamp for weeks.

17

Princess's hair had turned pink the moment she entered the Land of Fake-Believe.

I think it looks kind of cool.

The girls smiled at each other.

Then Princess's stomach let out a loud grumble.

GRUMBLE

Do you know where I can get something to eat?

I know just the place! Follow me!

Moldylocks grabbed Princess's hand.
Princess had to run to keep up.

CHAPTER THREE
A Zany House

Here we are!

Moldylocks stopped in front of one of the strangest houses Princess had ever seen. It looked like several normal houses had been mixed up in a giant blender. No two windows or doors were the same.

Let's see if they are home.

Let's see if who is home?

The Three Beards.

You mean the three <u>bears</u>?

No, no— the Three <u>Beards</u>. They're much scarier than bears.

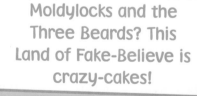

Moldylocks and the Three Beards? This Land of Fake-Believe is crazy-cakes!

23

Princess and Moldylocks tiptoed through the front door.

Inside, there was a long wooden table. There were three chairs at the table. In front of each chair was a bowl of chili.

Princess scrambled up onto the first chair. It was way too soft.

Let's try another chair.

The second chair was way too hard.

This stinks. How about we try that last chair?

The third chair was covered in sticky honey and piles of hair.

Maybe we should forget the chairs and eat standing up.

Princess took a big spoonful of the first bowl of chili.

BRRR! This chili is way too cold.

Moldylocks took a big spoonful of the second bowl of chili.

YEEOW! This chili is way too hot!

Then Princess and Moldylocks took a big spoonful of chili from the third bowl. It was just right.

The Beards always have the best chili!

Princess was about to take another bite, when she saw something move inside the bowl. She leaned in for a closer look.

A spider popped out from the middle of the chili!

29

Princess wasn't sure
this was a good idea.
But she followed
Moldylocks up the
stairs anyway.

· CHAPTER FOUR ·
A Comfy Bed

When Princess and Moldylocks reached the top of the stairs, they were both out of breath. It was a long way up!

The girls went into the first room they found. There were three beds in the room. Princess got an idea.

Let's play Cowboy Caveman!

These beds look perfect for jumping on while we hunt dinosaurs. What do you say?

GRaaaaahhhHHH!

The girls hopped up onto the first bed. It was way too soft.

What an awful bed!

We can't jump on this bed! It feels like a mushy banana! Let's try the second bed.

The second bed wasn't any better.

We can't jump on this bed! It's WAY too hard!

How can one room have so many awful beds in it?

Maybe we'll have luck with the last bed.

The girls touched the soft blanket on
the third bed.

They were about to jump up onto
the perfect bed when Princess heard
something.

Reggie was in the bed, wearing purple bunny pajamas. He wasn't alone. There were many spiders sleeping in the bed. Too many to count!

**Princess yawned. Then Moldylocks
yawned, too.**

All those snoring spiders
are making me sleepy.

That first bed was too
soft for jumping,
but it'd be perfect
for napping.

**The girls fell fast asleep in the small,
squishy bed.**

Princess and Moldylocks woke up with a start. They could hear angry voices coming from downstairs.

ARGGH! WHO HAS BEEN SITTING IN OUR CHAIRS?

WHO HAS BEEN EATING OUR CHILI?

The girls could hear clomping on the stairs. The Beards were getting closer and closer and closer!

· CHAPTER FIVE ·
Three Angry Beards

Hey, Mama Beard! Has my bed always looked so lumpy and bumpy?

That no-good spider and all of his cousins had better not be napping in it again!

Papa Beard yanked the blanket back to find out who was sleeping in Baby Beard's bed.

Princess could see that the creatures
were three walking, talking beards with
arms and legs. And all three of them were

Princess grabbed Moldylocks by the hand. The girls ran to the stairway. The Three Beards chased after them, clawing at the air with their long arms.

RUN!

Princess let go of Moldylocks's hand. Then she slid down the banister as fast as she could.

Princess didn't stop running until she was outside, with the Beards's house far behind her.

Moldylocks was nowhere to be seen. Princess looked over her shoulder just in time to see Mama and Papa Beard snatching up her friend.

And Baby Beard was running toward Princess.

EEK!

Princess ran and ran—until she was standing below the door that led out of Fake-Believe.

Mother Moose was riding a bizarre animal. It looked like a unicorn, but instead of a horn, it had a tuna fish on its head.

Hurry! Baby Beard is right behind you! Tunacorn can fly! She'll take you up to the door!

Tunacorn swooped Princess up into the air just as Baby Beard came barreling toward them.

Thanks for your help!

Princess scrambled through the door.

She slammed it behind her. Then she sat down on the cold kitchen floor, catching her breath.

Princess had escaped the Three Beards. She had made it out of the Land of Fake-Believe. But she had left Moldylocks in the paws of the Three Beards!

Princess got a terrible feeling in her tummy. She knew she had to go back to Fake-Believe. Princess <u>had</u> to save her new friend from the Three Beards!
So Princess came up with a plan.

Then she stepped through her fridge.

· CHAPTER SIX ·
A Strange Visitor

Princess fell back down into the Land of Fake-Believe. Then she ran as fast as she could to the Three Beards's house.

Princess peeked through the Beards's
kitchen window.

The Three Beards were lowering poor
Moldylocks into a giant, bubbling pot
of chili! Reggie and his cousins were
swimming in the chili.

You Beards don't <u>really</u> want to eat me, do you? I'm pretty moldy.

This is the best chili bath EVER!

Baby Beard was busily adding spices to the pot. A beach ball bonked Moldylocks on the nose. Princess knew she had to do something fast!

There was a very loud knock on the
front door of the Three Beards's house.

The Three Beards stared at one another. None of them could remember having a grandpa named Beardo the Weirdo.

All Three Beards opened the door. They were knocked over as the visitor barged in.

I NEED A HOT BATH AFTER SUCH A LONG TRIP! WHAT ARE YOU THREE FUR-BRAINS STANDING AROUND FOR?! GET MY BATH READY!! AND THERE HAD BETTER BE A RUBBER DUCKIE IN IT!!

The Three Beards tripped over one another to get out of there.

Papa Beard ran to the bathroom to get the bath ready.

Mama Beard ran to the bedroom to get the pajamas.

And Baby Beard ran to the basement to hide.

They would have done anything to make the big, mean beard stop yelling.

While the Three Beards were racing around, Grandpa Beardo slowly walked over to the giant chili pot. He took a big sniff and patted his round belly.

Please don't eat me, sir.

Why would I eat my new friends? Come on! We have to get out of here!

The giant beard was Princess Pink!

Moldylocks was so happy. She gave Princess a chili-soaked hug.

The two girls jumped out the kitchen window and ran away as fast as they could. Reggie and his cousins toweled themselves off. Then they went to find somewhere to sleep.

Princess Pink and Moldylocks ran all the way to the door in the sky. Mother Moose was there. He was tying a ladder to the door.

65

Princess climbed up the ladder. She looked at her new friends.

I promise to come back soon!

When Princess closed the fridge,
it started humming again.

She opened the door once more.
Everything was back where it belonged.
The green-bean casserole was next to
the mustard with the crusty lid.

Princess gobbled up the green-bean casserole.

Then she smiled, thinking about the Land of Fake-Believe.

Could the Land of Fake-Believe have been a dream?

Now that her belly was full, all she <u>really</u> wanted to do was go to sleep.

Princess flopped down facefirst onto her bed.

She barely noticed the snoring spide
on the pillow next to her.

Noah Z. Jones

is an author, illustrator, and animator who creates all sorts of zany characters. He couldn't wait to dig up some of his weirdest creations yet for the Land of Fake-Believe! Noah has illustrated many books for children, including *Always in Trouble*, *Not Norman*, and *Those Shoes*. Princess Pink and the Land of Fake-Believe is the first children's book series that Noah has both written and illustrated.

How well do you know THE LAND OF FAKE-BELIEVE?

Look at the picture of the Land of Fake-Believe on pages 20 and 21. How is it different from the world you know?

How is the story of **Moldylocks and the Three Beards** similar to and different from **Goldilocks and the Three Bears**?

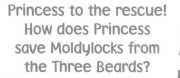

Princess to the rescue! How does Princess save Moldylocks from the Three Beards?

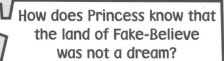

How does Princess know that the land of Fake-Believe was not a dream?

Use words and pictures to create a story similar to **Moldylocks and the Three Beards** and **Goldilocks and the Three Bears**. Include something that is too soft, something that is too hard, and something that is just right.